The Berenstain Bears®
Gifts of the Spirit

JOYFUL CELEBRATION
ACTIVITY BOOK

Mike Berenstain

Random House 🏠 New York

Based on the characters created by Stan and Jan Berenstain

Welcome!

This is the Bear family—Mama, Papa, Brother, Sister, and Honey. What's your name?

Write it in the space below.

My name is

_____.

A New Arrival

The Bear family is celebrating
the birth of baby Teddi!

Solve the maze to help Gran and Gramps
get to the celebration.

See answers on page 32.

Favorite Time of Year

Follow the lines to find out each cub's favorite holiday.
Circle the holiday that you like best!

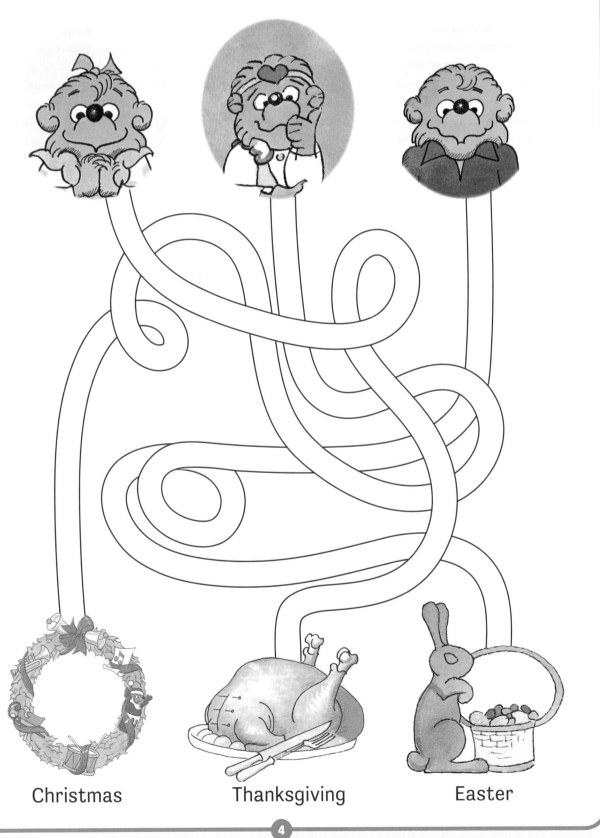

Christmas   Thanksgiving   Easter

4

There It Is!

Brother and Sister just found
the perfect birthday present for Mama.

What do you think makes a good gift?
Draw it below!

A Better Letter

Brother is working on a special birthday card.
Decorate it, and write something nice, too.

Party Planners

Find and circle the words in the list below.
They can be found forward and down.

Word Bank

BALLOONS

DANCE

EAT

FOOD

FUN

LAUGH

PLAY

SHARE

SING

O B F B A X S F

D A N C E K H O

S L J F A L X O

H L A U G H R D

S O F N S O E K

I O K U P L A Y

N N C Q U S T J

G S H A R E I E

7

Come Join Us

There's going to be a neighborhood party.

Decorate this sign to let everyone know about it.

Present Patterns

Use the stickers in this book to
complete the pattern in each row below.

    _____

   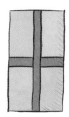 _____

_____

 _____

 _____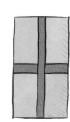

See answers on page 32.

Egg Excitement

Brother and Sister are going on an Easter egg hunt!

Find and circle all the eggs.

See answers on page 32.

Double Discovery

Can you spot the matching pictures of Brother and Sister?

Circle the two pictures that are exactly alike.

A

B

C

D

See answers on page 32.

Eggs-actly

Draw a line between the matching eggs below.

See answers on page 32.

Church Search

Find and circle the six things that are different
in the bottom picture.

13

Birthday Bash

It's Cousin Fred's birthday.

Help the Bear family decorate a special cake for him.

Party Time

Use the pictures as clues to find the correct words for the crossword puzzle below. Then use the word bank to complete the puzzle.

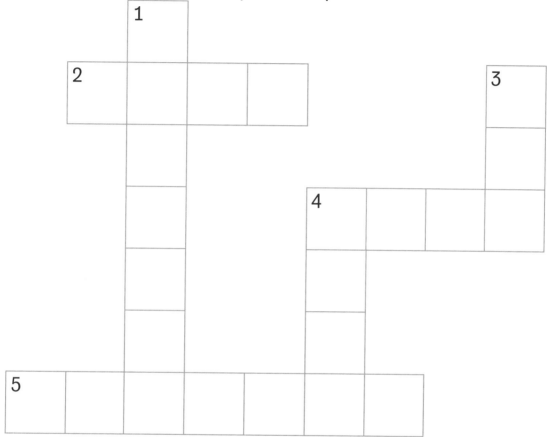

Across:

2

4

5

Down:

1

3

4

Word Bank

BALLOON   CAKE   CANDLES   GAME   GIFT   HAT

See answers on page 32.

School Success

Finish this picture of Sister at her graduation.

Twin Treats

Can you find the two pictures that are exactly alike?

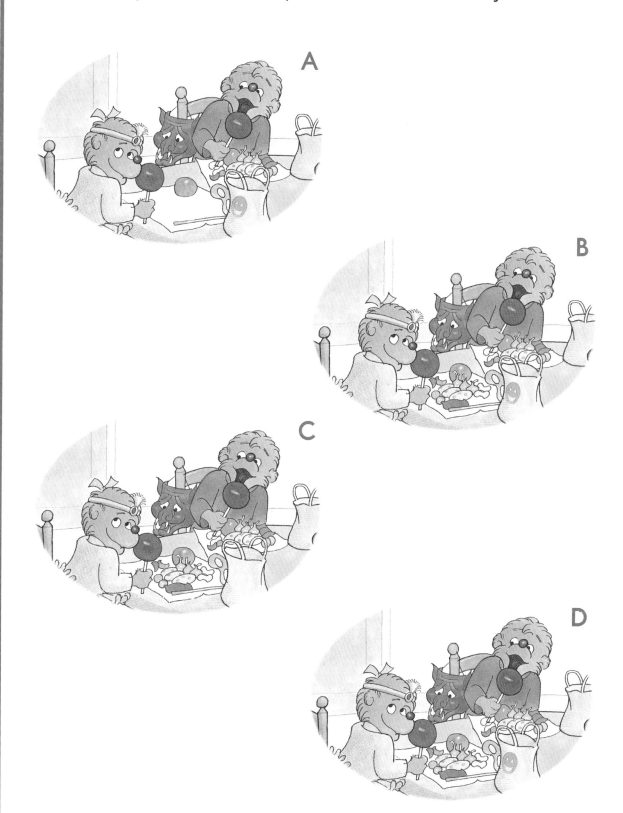

A

B

C

D

See answers on page 32.

Make a Mask

Create a holiday disguise.

Color and use stickers to
decorate this mask.

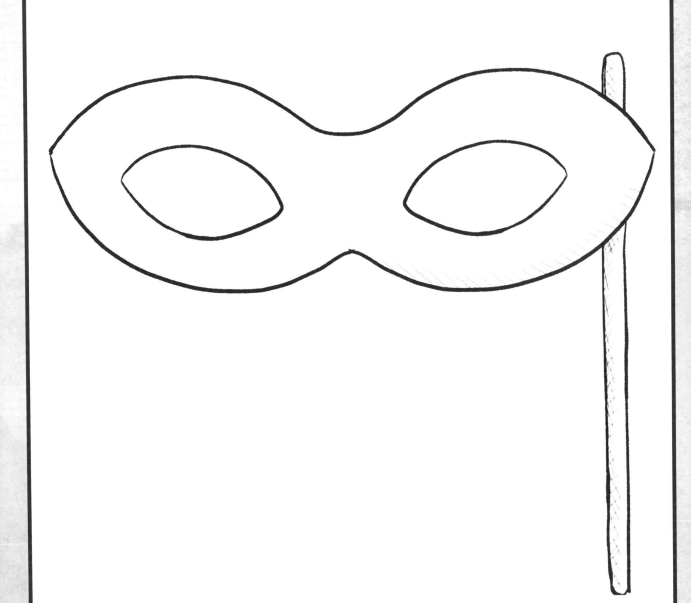

Halloween Hunt

Find and circle the words in the list below.
They can be found forward and down.

Word Bank

BOO

CANDY

COSTUME

FUN

MASK

PUMPKIN

SPOOKY

TREAT

TRICK

R F S P O O K Y

O I C O B F U N

T B O O R Q J K

R E S M A S K C

I H T L O R E A

C P U M P K I N

K H M G N F E D

T R E A T E M Y

See answers on page 32.

Exciting Events

The Bear family loves to celebrate together.

Draw lines to the items that match each celebration.

Graduation

Birthday

Easter

Halloween

Christmas

See answers on page 32.

What to Bring?

The Bear family is going to the neighborhood potluck.

Circle the things that they could bring for others to eat. Then put an X on the things that would not be so tasty.

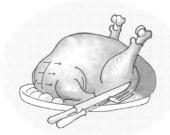

See answers on page 32.

Snow Day!

Unscramble the words below.
Use the word bank if you need help.

GESIHL _____

LPYA _____

GNLAE _____

RFTO _____

NTMEIST _____

RAZBLZDI _____

NSWO _____

DLCO _____

Word Bank	ANGEL	BLIZZARD	COLD	FORT
	MITTENS	SLEIGH	SNOW	PLAY

See answers on page 32.

Fresh Frost

Sister is looking out the window at the first snowfall of the year.

Decorate this page with snowflakes.

Special Guest

Use the numbers to color this picture of a special visitor.

1 = ⬛ 2 = ⬜ 3 = ⬛ 4 = ⬜ 5 = ⬛

See answers on page 32.

Dear Santa

Sister is writing a letter to Santa!

Use the word bank to complete her letter.

D_____ Santa,

C_____ will be here soon.

It's my favorite h_____.

I've been g_____ this year.

I hope you will bring me a p_____.

See you s_____!

Word Bank

CHRISTMAS   DEAR   GOOD   HOLIDAY   PRESENT   SOON

See answers on page 32.

Christmas Cheer

Find and circle the words in the list below.
They can be found forward and down.

K G A T R E E R R

P E L Q N S X M

J E S U S T G F

H J A V T A B O

M A N G E R A M

O Y T H Z K B J

I F A M I L Y O

R B U P M I R Y

Word Bank

BABY

FAMILY

JESUS

JOY

MANGER

SANTA

STAR

TREE

26

See answers on page 32.

Gift Guide

Brother and Sister are off to visit Santa.

Put the story in order by numbering the events from 1 to 4.

See answers on page 32.

Marvelous Morning

Color this picture of the Bear family on Christmas morning.

Then decorate it with stickers.

Holiday Homes

Everyone is decorating for the holidays.

Find and circle the six things that are
different in the bottom picture.

See answers on page 32.

Find the Festival

Solve the maze to help the Bear family get to the New Year's Eve party.

START

FINISH

See answers on page 32.

See You Again Soon!

Celebrate a new year. May it be filled with family time and fun.

Decorate this sign for the Bear family's New Year's celebration.

Answers

Page 3:

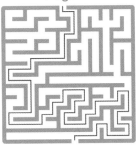

Page 4:

Christmas Thanksgiving Easter

Page 7:

```
O B F B A X S F
D A N C E K H O
S L J F A L X O
H L A U G H R D
S O F N S O E K
I O K U P L A Y
N C Q U S T J
G S H A R E I E
```

Page 9:

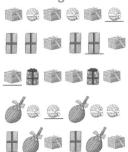

Page 10:

Page 11:

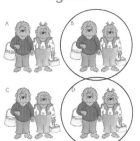

Page 12:

Page 13:

Page 15:

```
        ¹B
²C A K E         ³H
    L             A
    L      ⁴G I F T
    O       A
    O       M
⁵C A N D L E S
```

Page 17:

Page 19:

```
R F S P O O K Y
O I C O B F U N
T B O O R Q J K
R E S M A S K C
I H T L O R E A
C P U M P K I N
K H M G N F E D
T R E A T E M Y
```

Page 20:

Graduation	
Birthday	
Easter	
Halloween	
Christmas	

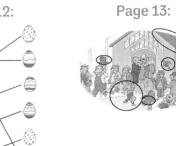

Page 21:

Page 22:

GESIHL	SLEIGH
LPYA	PLAY
GNLAE	ANGEL
RFTO	FORT
NTMEIST	MITTENS
RAZBLZDI	BLIZZARD
NSWO	SNOW
DLCO	COLD

Page 24:

Page 25:

Dear Santa.

Christmas will be here soon.

It's my favorite holiday.

I've been good this year.

I hope you will bring me a present.

See you soon!

Page 26:

```
K G A T R E E R
P E L Q N S X M
J E S U S T G F
H J A V T A B O
M A N G E R R M
O Y T H Z K B J
I F A M I L Y O
R B U P M I R Y
```

Page 27:

Page 29:

Page 30: